The
ELEPHANT's
Child

For Nicola, who made these books look Just So!

Find out more about
Rudyard Kipling's
JUST so STORIES

at Shoo Rayner's fabulous website,

www.shoo-rayner.co.uk

First published in 2007 by Orchard Books
First paperback publication in 2008

ORCHARD BOOKS
338 Euston Road, London NW1 3BH
Orchard Books Australia
Level 17/207 Kent St, Sydney, NSW 2000

ISBN 978 1 84616 406 4 (hardback)
ISBN 978 1 84616 414 9 (paperback)

A CIP catalogue record for this book is available from the British Library.

1 3 5 7 9 10 8 6 4 2 (hardback)
1 3 5 7 9 10 8 6 4 2 (paperback)

Printed in England by Antony Rowe Ltd, Chippenham, Wiltshire

Orchard Books is a division of Hachette Children's Books,
an Hachette Livre UK company.

www.orchardbooks.co.uk

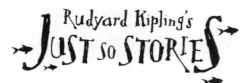

Rudyard Kipling's
JUST SO STORIES

The
ELEPHANT'S
Child

Retold and illustrated by
SHOO RAYNER

ORCHARD BOOKS

Long, long ago, at the very beginning of time, when everything was just getting sorted out, the Elephant had only a stumpy, bulgy nose, as big as a boot.

He could wriggle it about from side to side, but he couldn't pick things up with it.

There was one Elephant – a new Elephant – an Elephant's Child – who was full of insatiable curiosity, which made him ask ever so many questions.

He asked his broad aunt, the Hippopotamus, why her eyes were red.

And he asked his hairy uncle, the Baboon, why melons tasted so good. But none of them paid him any attention.

He asked questions about everything that he saw, or heard, or felt, or smelt, or touched.

No one paid him any attention, but he was still full of insatiable curiosity!

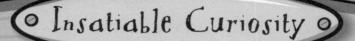

Insatiable Curiosity

Insatiable: means a hunger that cannot be satisfied.

Curiosity: means to have a hunger to know about something.

How much?

Why?

What?

How?

When?

What for?

What if?

The Elephant's Child had such a hunger for knowledge, he could never be satisfied with the answers he got!

One fine morning the insatiable
Elephant's Child asked, "What does the
Crocodile have for dinner?"

Everybody said, "Hush!" and paid
him no more attention.

But the Kolokolo Bird said, with
a mournful cry, "Go to the banks of
the great grey-green, greasy Limpopo
River, all set about with fever-trees,
and find out."

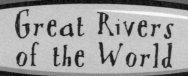

Great Rivers of the World

The Limpopo is in Southern Africa. It is sometimes known as the Crocodile River.

The Limpopo is very slow. It ends at the port of Xai Xai in the Indian Ocean in the country of Mozambique.

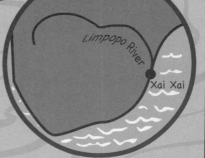

Limpopo River

Xai Xai

The very next morning,
the insatiable Elephant's
Child packed a hundred
pounds of bananas,

a hundred
pounds of
sugar-cane

and seventeen
melons.

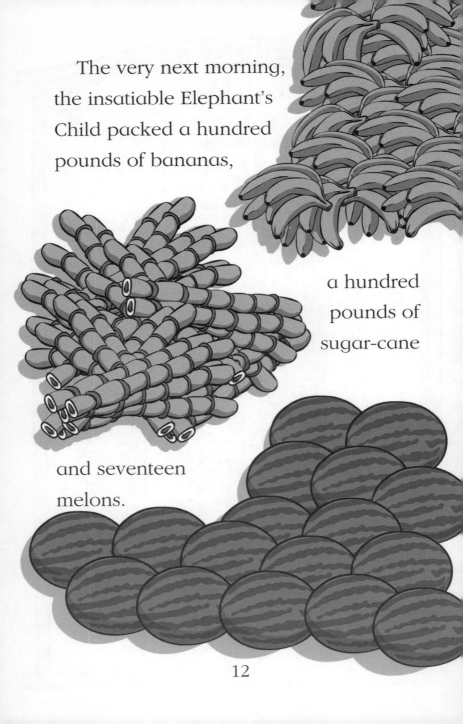

He said to his dear family, who paid him no attention, "Goodbye. I am going to the great grey-green, greasy Limpopo River, all set about with fever-trees, to find out what the Crocodile has for dinner."

He went on his way, eating all the time, and throwing the skins about, because he could not pick them up.

At last he came to the banks of the great grey-green, greasy Limpopo River, all set about with fever-trees, precisely as the Kolokolo Bird had said.

Now you must know and understand that this insatiable Elephant's Child had never seen a Crocodile, and did not know what one was like.

The first thing he found was
a Bi-Coloured-Python-Rock-Snake
curled round a rock.

"Excuse me," said the Elephant's
Child most politely, "but have you seen
a Crocodile in these parts?"

"Have I seen a Crocodile?" said the
Bi-Coloured-Python-Rock-Snake, in
a voice of dreadful scorn. "What will
you ask me next?"

"Excuse me," said the Elephant's
Child most politely, "but could you
kindly tell me what he has for dinner?"

The Bi-Coloured-Python-Rock-Snake
uncoiled himself, turned his back to the
sun and paid him no more attention.

The Elephant's Child said goodbye
very politely and went on his way,
eating melons, and throwing the rind
about because he could not pick it up.

Then, at the very edge of the great grey-green, greasy Limpopo River, all set about with fever-trees, he trod on what he thought was a log.

But it was really the Crocodile, who winked one eye!

"Excuse me," said the
Elephant's Child most politely,
"but do you happen to have
seen a Crocodile in these parts?"

The Crocodile winked the
other eye, and lifted half his tail
out of the mud.

"Come closer,
Little One," said the
Crocodile. "Why do
you ask such things?"

"Excuse me," said the Elephant's Child most politely, pleased that someone was paying attention. "No one else will answer me."

"Come closer, Little One," said the Crocodile, "for I am the Crocodile," and he wept crocodile-tears to show it was quite true.

The Elephant's Child grew excited and kneeled down on the bank and said, "You are the very person I have been looking for. Will you please tell me what you have for dinner?"

"Come closer, Little One," said the Crocodile, "and I'll whisper."

The Elephant's Child put his head down close to the Crocodile's musky, tusky mouth, and the Crocodile caught him by his little nose, which up to that moment, had been no bigger than a boot, and just about as useful.

"I think," said the Crocodile, through gritted teeth, "I think today I will begin with Elephant's Child!"

The Elephant's Child was much annoyed, and he spoke through his nose, "Led go! You are hurting be!"

25

Then the Bi-Coloured-Python-Rock-Snake scuffled down the bank and said, "Pull as hard as ever you can, or he'll pull you into those grey-green, greasy waters before you can say Jack Robinson."

The Elephant's Child sat back
on his little haunches, and pulled,
and pulled, and pulled, and his
nose began to stretch.

The Crocodile floundered in the
water, making it all creamy with
great sweeps of his tail, and he
pulled, and pulled, and pulled.

The Elephant's Child spread all his little four legs and pulled, and pulled, and pulled, and his nose kept on stretching.

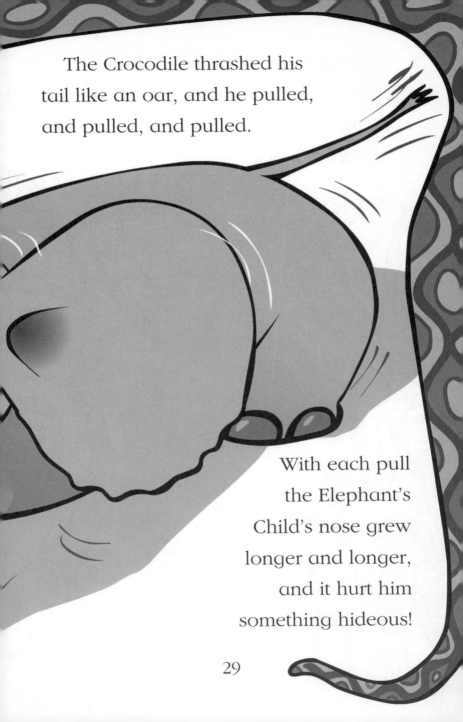

The Crocodile thrashed his tail like an oar, and he pulled, and pulled, and pulled.

With each pull the Elephant's Child's nose grew longer and longer, and it hurt him something hideous!

29

The Elephant's Child felt his legs
slipping, and he said through his nose,
which was now nearly five feet long,
"This is too butch for be!"

Then the Bi-Coloured-
Python-Rock-Snake knotted
himself in a double-clove-hitch
round the Elephant's
Child's back legs,
and pulled.

The Crocodile pulled
and pulled but the
Elephant's Child and
the Bi-Coloured-
Python-Rock-Snake
pulled hardest.

31

At last the
Crocodile let
go of the
Elephant's
Child's nose
with a plop
that you
could hear all
up and down
the Limpopo.

PLOP!

The Elephant's Child wrapped his nose up in cool banana leaves, and hung it in the great grey-green, greasy Limpopo to cool.

He sat there for three days waiting for his nose to shrink. But it never grew any shorter.

At the end of the third day a fly stung him on the shoulder, and before he knew what he was doing he lifted up his trunk and squashed that fly with the end of it.

"Advantage number one!" said the Bi-Coloured-Python-Rock-Snake. "You couldn't have done that with a mere-smear nose. Try and eat a little now."

35

The Elephant's Child
put out his trunk and
plucked a large bundle
of grass, dusted it clean
against his forelegs, and
stuffed it into his mouth.

"Advantage number two!" said
the Bi-Coloured-Python-Rock-
Snake. "You couldn't have done
that with a mere-smear nose. Don't
you think the sun is very hot?"

"It is," said the Elephant's Child, putting out his trunk and schlooping up a schloop of mud from the banks of the great grey-green, greasy Limpopo.

He slapped it on his head, where it made a cool schloopy-sloshy mud-cap all trickly behind his ears.

"Advantage number three!" said the Bi-Coloured-Python-Rock-Snake. "You couldn't have done that with a mere-smear nose."

So the Elephant's Child went home across Africa frisking and whisking his trunk. When he wanted to eat he pulled fruit down from a tree, and when he wanted grass he plucked it up from the ground.

He felt so happy, he sang to himself down his trunk, and the noise was louder than several brass bands.

Brass Bands

Instruments you will find in a brass band.

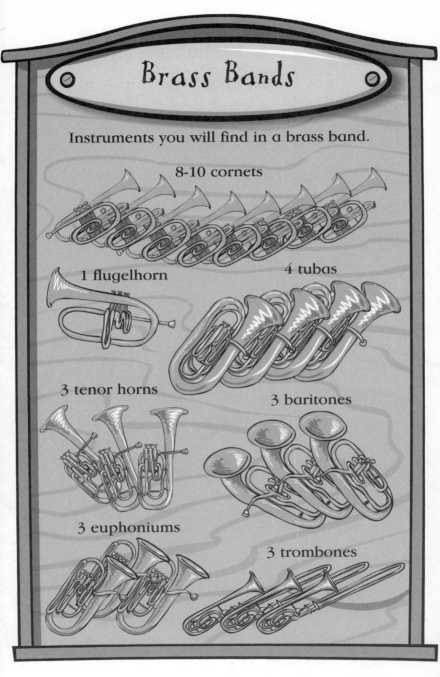

8-10 cornets

1 flugelhorn

4 tubas

3 tenor horns

3 baritones

3 euphoniums

3 trombones

One dark evening he came back
to his dear family, who ignored him
and paid him no attention, even
though he'd been away.

He coiled up his trunk and blew
so loud and so long, they had to
pay attention.

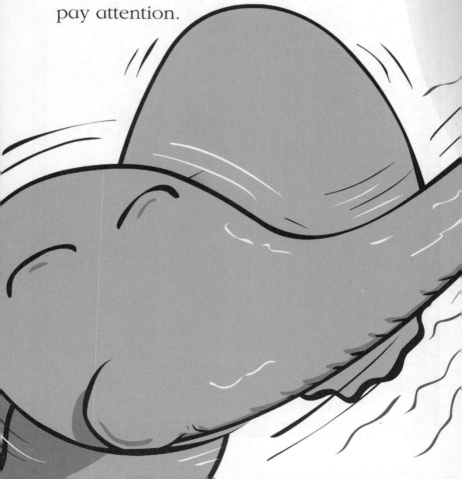

"O Bananas!" they
said. "Where did you
learn that trick, and
what have you done
to your nose?"

43

"I got a new one from the Crocodile on the banks of the great grey-green, greasy Limpopo River," said the Elephant's Child. "I asked him what he had for dinner, and he gave me this to keep."

Then he showed off all the things he could do with his nose, while his family paid him close attention.

Things You Can Do With Your Nose

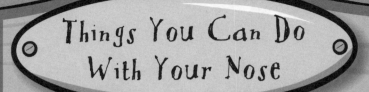

Sneeze

Smell flowers

Sniff in a loud and annoying manner

Wiggle your nostrils – try it!

Scrunch it up

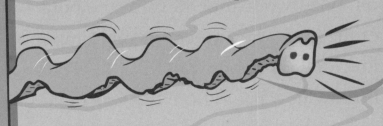

They were so excited that they went
off, one by one in a hurry, to the banks
of the great grey-green, greasy Limpopo
River, all set about with fever-trees, to
borrow new noses from the Crocodile.

Ever since that day all the Elephants
you will ever see, besides all those that
you won't, have trunks precisely like the
trunk of the insatiably curious
Elephant's Child.

Rudyard Kipling's
JUST SO STORIES

Retold and illustrated by
SHOO RAYNER

All priced at £8.99

Rudyard Kipling's Just So Stories are available from all good bookshops,
or can be ordered direct from
the publisher: Orchard Books, PO BOX 29, Douglas IM99 1BQ
Credit card orders please telephone 01624 836000
or fax 01624 837033 or visit our internet site: www.orchardbooks.co.uk
or e-mail: bookshop@enterprise.net for details.

To order please quote title, author and ISBN
and your full name and address.
Cheques and postal orders should be made payable to 'Bookpost plc.'
Postage and packing is FREE within the UK
(overseas customers should add £2.00 per book).

Prices and availability are subject to change.